Zzzz

This book belongs to:

_____

(you are AWESOME!)

Good Night
my little MU bird™

Dear James,
May you always
feel safe, warm
and cozy :♡:
love, Angie DeMuro

A Land of MU™ storybook
USA

written and illustrated by
Angie DeMuro

This book was manufactured in the USA

Printing by:

Nick of Time Printing LLC, 2931 Memorial Hwy., Dallas, PA. 18612
www.nickoftimeprinting.com

Editor: Douglas C. Burak

"Good Night my little MU bird"

ISBN   978-0-9885568-3-6

0988556836

Visit Angie and the MU birds™ at

www.angiedemuro.com

This book is dedicated to my father, Joseph DeMuro.

Thank you for your bedtime stories; they were always fantastical and funny and have allowed my imagination to soar.

● ● ● ● ● ● ● ● ● ● ● ● ● ● ● ● ● ●

I thank my three MU birds, Dominic, Nicholas and Michael... you are my heart and one of my biggest purposes for being.

I thank my best friend/ husband/ critic/ editor/ biggest fan, Douglas. Your belief in me is empowering and your encouragement is never ending; for without you I would not hold this book in my hands.

Milo MU was having such a FUN day!

It was filled with many adventures
and lots of pretend play...

Super Milo

King Milo

Rockin' Milo

Detective Milo

Artist Milo

Space Milo

Soon the round moon appeared
up in the sky.

A sure sign that the day
had indeed
flown by.

Daddy MU bird said,
"It looks like our day has come
to an end.

Time to clean up,
and get ready for bed."

So clean up Milo did,
putting all his toys back
on the shelves.

Daddy MU bird came in
and gave him some help.

"Into the tub" says Daddy,
"It is time for your bath."

"YAY" yells Milo.

Because he likes to...

Milo gets out, dries off and
puts his jammies on.

Now he feels so cozy and warm!

It is time for Milo's favorite
bedtime treat.

A bit of bread and honey...

It makes him so happy he lets out
a little tweet!

When Milo is done, he asks,

"Daddy what book will you read?"

Daddy MU bird says,
"Oh, not until you brush your
little MU bird beak."

Milo climbed up into bed
so tired and clean...

as Daddy MU bird sat down
and started to read.

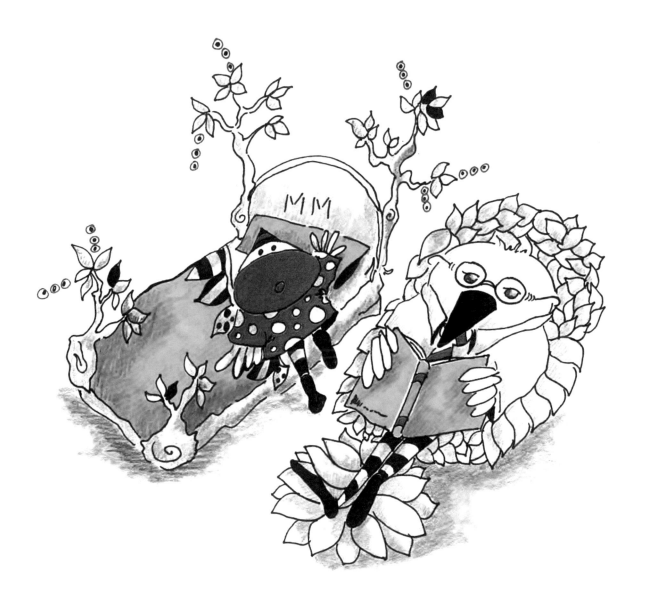

And by the time Daddy MU bird was
done reading for the night,

Milo MU bird's eyes
were already shut very tight.

Daddy MU bird leaned over
and gave Milo a kiss on the beak...

And Milo opened one eye and
gave his Daddy a little wink.

Daddy MU bird whispered as he left Milo's room…

"Good Night my little MU, for tomorrow another adventure waits for you."

GOOD NIGHT!

The End